RITA & RALPH'S

WRITTEN BY Carmen Agra Deedy

ROTTEN DAY

ILLUSTRATED BY Pete Oswald

SCHOLASTIC INC.

In two little houses,

on two little hills,

lived two best friends.

Every morning, Rita and Ralph would

open their doors,

step outside,

close their doors,

and run . . .

. . . down the hill,   and up the hill,

and down the hill, and up the hill.

They'd meet under the apple tree and high-five,

pinkie-shake,

do a cha-cha-cha,

play zombie tag,

and make daisy chains.

Then one day . . .

they played a *new* game:

Sticks and Stones.

"Oooooow!" yowled Rita.

"UH-OH." Ralph froze.

This was bad.

Really bad.

So they ran away . . .

. . . down the hill,   and up the hill,

and down the hill, and up the hill.

They opened their doors,

raced inside,

and closed their doors.

Rita was mad.

And Ralph was . . . sorry.

So Ralph opened the door,

stepped outside,

and closed the door.

It was a hundred years to Rita's house.

But she was his best friend.

So Ralph went . . .

down the hill, and up the hill, and down the hill, and up the hill,

and down the hill, and up the hill, and down the hill, aaaaand up the hill.

The long walk made Ralph

a smidge grumpy.

"I'M SORRY!" he barked.

But he
didn't sound
one bit sorry.

So Rita did NOT

open the door.

"Grrrrrrr,"

said Ralph.

And off

he stomped . . .

. . . down the hill, and up the hill, and down the hill, and up the hill,

and down the hill,

and up the hill,

and down the hill,

aaaaand up the hill.

He opened the door,

stepped inside,

and closed the door.

Now Ralph was mad.

And Rita was . . . *kinda* sorry.

So she opened the door,

stepped outside,

closed the door,

and ran . . .

. . . down the hill, and up the hill, and down the hill, and up the hill, and down the hill, and up the hill, and down the hill, aaaaand up the hill.

As she ran,

she thought about Ralph.

And that rock.

Just thinking about it

made her mad

all over again.

"I WANT MY PINECONE BACK!"

she shouted.

Ralph opened the door,

and closed the door.

And Rita tromped . . .

down the hill, and up the hill, and down the hill, and up the hill,

and down the hill,

and up the hill,

and down the hill,

aaaaand up the hill.

She opened her door,

marched inside,

and slammed the door.

Now Rita was mad.

And Ralph was mad.

And Rita was sad.

And Ralph was sad.

And in two little houses on two little hills, no one slept a wink.

It had been a rotten day.

Just when it seemed

nothing would be right again,

it was a new day.

Rita and Ralph

opened their doors,

stepped outside,

closed their doors,

and went . . .

. . . down the hill,   and up the hill,

and down the hill, and up the hill.

"I'm sorry!" said Rita.

"I'm sorrier!" said Ralph.

And they meant it.

They did a high five,

and a pinkie shake,

and a cha-cha-cha,

and played zombie tag,

and made daisy chains.

Because best friends *always* find a way . . .

. . . to meet in the middle.

101 THINGS
TO BUILD
with a little help
from your friends

Note from the Author

Most of us have said and done things
we regret. Nothing feels worse, however,
than hurting a friend. Breaking things
takes little effort; mending them takes
time, humility, and a heap of trips up
and down the hills of reconciliation.

This story, inspired by the classic hand
game, "Mr. Wiggle & Mr. Waggle,"
may be read aloud with the accompanying
hand gestures on this page. You may
even want to add a few of your own!

 1. In two little houses on two little hills

 2. They opened the door

 3. They stepped outside

 4. And they closed the door

 5. They went down the hill

 6. They went up the hill

 7. And they met in the middle

ISBN 978-1-338-66069-2

10 9 8 7 6 5 4 3   21 22 23 24

Printed in the U.S.A.   40 • First printing 2020

For my
grandchildren,
Ruby,
Sam,
Grace,
Brady,
and
Chloe.
— C.D.

For
Nini
— P.O.

Special thanks — to Sherry Norfolk,
educator, storyteller,
and most generous friend. — C.D.

Pete Oswald's illustrations were rendered digitally using gouache watercolor textures.
The text type was set in Futura Medium. • The display type was set in Khaki Std 1.
Production was overseen by Catherine Weening. • Manufacturing was supervised by Shannon Rice.
The book was art directed and designed by Marijka Kostiw, and edited by Dianne Hess.